First published 1992 by Walker Books Ltd
87 Vauxhall Walk, London SE11 5HJ

This edition published 2009

2 4 6 8 10 9 7 5 3 1

© 1992 Michelle Cartlidge

The right of Michelle Cartlidge to be identified as author/illustrator
of this work has been asserted by her in accordance with the
Copyright, Designs and Patents Act 1988

This book has been typeset in Garamond Educational

Printed in China

British Library Cataloguing in Publication Data:
a catalogue record for this book is available from the British Library.

ISBN 978-0-7445-1691-3

www.walker.co.uk

Goodnight Teddy

Michelle Cartlidge

WALKER BOOKS
AND SUBSIDIARIES

LONDON • BOSTON • SYDNEY • AUCKLAND

Teddy loves to play
with his toys, but soon
it's time for bed.

"Bathtime!" calls Mummy Bear. Teddy takes his sailing boat, his duck and his favourite Pink Rabbit.

Teddy sails his boat
and Rabbit watches
from the chair.
"Don't forget to
wash, Teddy," says
Mummy Bear.

Teddy dries himself,
then he brushes his teeth
and is ready for bed.

Elephant, Mousey,
Moley and Pussycat
live in Teddy's
bedroom. But where
is Pink Rabbit?

Here comes Mummy
Bear. Look, she has
Pink Rabbit!
"Teddy, you left him
in the bathroom."

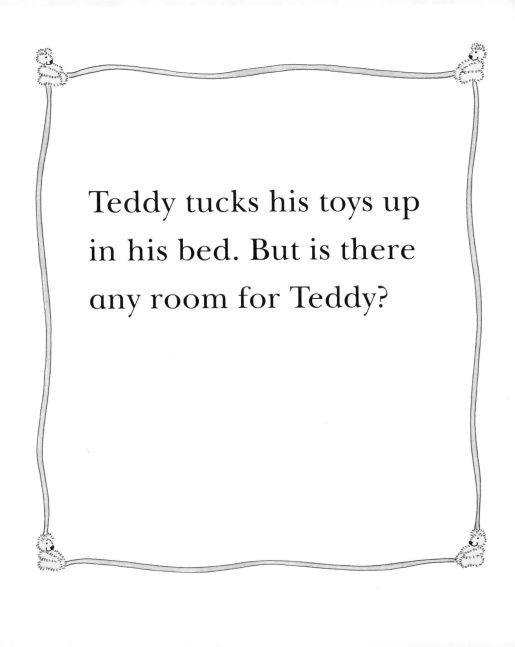

Teddy tucks his toys up in his bed. But is there any room for Teddy?

"Goodnight, Teddy," whispers Mummy Bear, "and dream sweet dreams."